THE RIGHTFUL OWNER

THE RIGHTFUL OWNER

JESSE STUART

EDITED BY

JIM WAYNE MILLER
JERRY A. HERNDON
JAMES M. GIFFORD

ORIGINAL ILLUSTRATIONS
BY ROBERT HENNEBERGER
BOOK DESIGN
BY ROCKY ZORNES

THE JESSE STUART FOUNDATION

ISBN 0-945084-15-3

The Jesse Stuart Foundation
P.O. Box 391
Ashland, KY 41114
1991

Dedicated to
The Kentucky Jaycees

CONTENTS

Wild Dog In The Pasture

"Here, fellow, here!" Mike called, "Come here to me! I won't hurt you! I don't have a dog! I'd like to have you!"

The dog stood in the pasture field looking at Mike Richards. A rope was around his neck, with the loose end on the ground. He was a hound dog with ears so long and soft Mike could have tied them in a knot over or under his head. Mike had heard his father say that the best way to tell a good hound was by his long ears. This hound had ears so long they nearly reached the ground.

"All right, if you won't come to me, I'll come to you," Mike said. "Somebody has been mean to you or you wouldn't be afraid of me! Somebody has tied you with that rope!"

Mike began walking toward the hound. Now if he will just stand there long enough for me to get close enough to grab the end of that rope, Mike thought. He took one careful step at a time. He was getting very close. The dog's body was mostly tan, with scattered black spots. His ears were long and brown. His head was black, with brown spots above the eyes.

"You're a nice-looking hound." Mike spoke softly to the dog, since he was getting closer to the end of the rope. "You've got big black spots over your body. If I had you, I'd call you Speckles. That would be a good name for you. Wouldn't you like Speckles for a name?"

The dog raised his head higher until he sniffed the cool spring wind that blew past Mike.

"My name is Michael Richards," Mike talked on very softly to the hound. "Everybody calls me Mike."

When Mike got very close, the hound started backing away, his big, soft, brown eyes watching every move the boy made. Mike stopped still in his tracks.

"Now, if you're afraid of me, I won't come any closer," Mike told the hound. "I told you that I wouldn't hurt

you. I just want to take you home with me. I believe you're lost. I want you to have a home. And I want you for my own."

Star, the pretty red cow with a white spot on her forehead, stopped eating the tender spring fescue, peppered with green orchard grass and white daisies, to look at Mike and the wary hound dog with the rope around its neck. Daisy, Star's heifer, also stopped eating grass to look and listen. Buck and Steve, the two large steers, didn't pay any attention. They kept on biting the pasture grass with their large grass-stained teeth. They made rasping sounds like a crosscut saw cutting through a green log. They didn't have time to watch Mike trying to catch a hound. They were too busy filling their stomachs with the sweet, green grass.

"You must like cattle," Mike said. "I believe you're a lost dog hunting your master!"

The hound stopped backing away. He sniffed the spring wind again. Then he whined very sadly and began to howl. Mike stood as still as a stone listening to the mournful howls. He watched the hound lift his head higher into the wind until his eyes looked toward the late afternoon sky where the sun was beginning to drop down the bright horizon. The lost hound's howls were so loud and sounded so lonesome that Mike put his fingers in his ears to shut out the sound.

"You poor lost hound," Mike said. "You are crying for your master. I hope you can find him. Then you would be very happy. But if you never find him, I'd like to be your master. No master will ever be nicer to you than I will be! Come on, Speckles! Come here to me! Come to me, now! I've got to go home with the cows!"

Then Mike jumped to grab the end of the rope, but the hound was too quick for him. He leaped away like a wild rabbit springing from its nest when it sees a hunter with a gun. The hound ran into the green leafy woods at the pasture's edge. Star and Daisy stood watching until he was out of sight. Then Mike started driving the cows home.

"I wonder why that hound won't come to me," Mike said to himself. "If only I had taken a piece of bread with me!"

*   *   *

It was very late when Mike reached the house. His mother and father were already sitting at the supper table.

"What kept you so late, Mike?" Mr. Richards asked. "Now don't tell me you saw that strange hound again, the one with the rope around his neck?"

"Yes, I found him back there with the cattle, Dad," Mike said. "That's why I'm late. I've been talking to him and calling him Speckles. I've been trying to catch him."

"We thought you might have found that hound again, and we were right!" his mother said, smiling. "Your supper will be cold. You'd better sit right down."

"All right, Mom," Mike said. "Dad, what can I do? I want that dog more than any dog I've ever seen. I like him but he doesn't care for me."

"He must be a hound that was lost in a fox chase," his father said. "He's lost his owner and he doesn't know you. He'd be hard to capture, but we could try."

13

"Would you, Dad? Would you help me catch him?"

"Yes, Mike, I'll help you. I think I even have an idea how we could do it. But, Mike, there's one thing you've got to understand. Your Speckles is looking for his rightful owner. Even if we bring him home and he gets to love us, he won't stay if he finds his real master. A good hound dog never forgets his master. Are you sure you want to take that chance?"

"Oh, yes!" Mike said. "Anyway, maybe his real owner just brought him in an automobile and dropped him out on the highway. Some people do that."

"The owner of a good dog would never do that," his father said. "But eat your supper now. I'll see about this in the morning. I don't like the idea of that dog running around with that rope on his neck, anyway. He might get hung up and starve to death, or he might choke himself."

Setting A Trap

When Mike came home from school the next day, he was surprised to see his father working in the back yard. Jim Richards had just finished making a strange box. Mike had never seen anything like it.

"It's a trap, but it can't hurt your hound," his father said. "I wouldn't use a trap that would hurt him."

"Is this really a trap, Dad?" Mike said. "I thought a trap had steel jaws. How did you ever think of making a trap like this?"

"Well, when I was about your age, my father built a trap like this to catch the yellow jackets in our meadows so they couldn't sting the horses when he mowed the grass," Mr. Richards answered Mike. "His trap was a smaller one than this. All he had to do was set the funnel of the trap over the hole where the yellow jackets came from the ground. They went into the big end of the funnel and out through the little end into the wire-covered box. They couldn't find their way back through

15

the funnel."

"But how will Speckles go into that funnel?" Mike asked.

"Easy enough," his father replied. "We'll set the trap in the pasture among the pines. We will put bait in it. The hound will go through the funnel to get it. When he does, he can't get out of the trap until we take him out. If we catch that dog, we have to be smarter than he is. He's not any ordinary dog. He's a smart one."

"I am glad it won't hurt him, Dad," Mike said.

The trap was made in the shape of a big box. It was covered with strong close-meshed wire, except for the bottom, which was made of boards. In one end there was an open funnel that went back into the box. It was made of woven wire, too. All the dog had to do was walk back through it to get the food left in the box. When he went through the funnel, a small door closed after him.

"Now, here is where we will open the trap and take him out," Mike's father said.

Mr. Richards showed Mike how the top of the trap was fastened with hinges and hasps. He unfastened the hasp on either end and raised the lid to show Mike how it worked.

"It will be simple to get the dog out if we catch him," his father explained. "We can take him out or leave him in. I went to Blakesburg this morning to buy the wire, hinges, and hasps. I've worked the rest of the day making this."

"Dad, you're smart to make this," Mike said as he

stood close, looking at the trap with admiration. "I wonder if Speckles is still in the pasture?"

"He was this morning," his father said. "I rode back there, and I saw him run to the woods. He stopped once to look back at me. Then I spoke to him and he started running again. He ran into the shadows of the grove."

"We ought to have the trap back there now," Mike said.

"I've got Bess and Doc harnessed and hitched to the wagon," Mr. Richards said. "They are waiting out there in the barn entry. Take your books in the house and get some bait for the trap. Let's load the trap into the wagon and be on our way. We must work fast."

Mike gathered his books up from the grass and ran as fast as he could into the house. When he returned, he had a paper sack filled with the best food his mother could find. His father had gone to the barn and had driven the team with the jolt wagon up beside the cage. Now he laid the leather checklines across the seat and stepped down.

"It's not very heavy," his father said. "But it is large and will take up a lot of room. You get over on that side and I'll stay on this side and we'll lift it into the wagon bed."

Mike and his father loaded the cage with ease. Then his father climbed up into the wagon and Mike followed.

"Here, take these lines and drive, Mike," said his father. "I'll hold your sack."

Mike took the lines. He reined Bess and Doc toward the grove. Mike and his broad-shouldered father sat on the springy seat laughing and talking as Bess and Doc trotted along over the green pasture with their harness jingling in the wind like tiny bells.

"Dad, when we rode home on the school bus, I was telling everybody about finding this wild dog in our pasture," Mike said. "Everyone believed me but Junior Addington. He turned around and said, 'Mike, you never found a wild dog in your pasture. I don't believe you!'"

"What did you tell him?" his father asked.

"I told him he didn't have to believe me," Mike replied. "I told him I had named the dog Speckles and he was the prettiest hound I had ever seen."

"I wouldn't pay any attention to Junior Addington," Mr. Richards said.

"One of these days I hope to show him whether I found a dog or not," Mike said. "I get along with everybody at school and on the bus but Junior Addington. None of the others get along with him, either. He's always quarreling with somebody at school, and no one wants to sit beside him on the school bus."

When they reached the pine grove, they didn't see the hound. The cattle were not in sight, either.

"He's not here now, but he'll come back with the cattle," Mike said. "Don't you believe he will, Dad?"

"Yes, if he's not tied up with that rope," his father replied.

"Speckles has taken up with the cattle because he's lonesome," Mike said softly. "He knows the cattle won't try to bother him!"

"Let's set the trap so we can drive back home to supper," Mr. Richards said. "I think we might have your Speckles by morning."

"If I could make a wish for what I want most in the

19

world, it would be that dog, Dad," Mike told him.

"Son, let's get out and lift the trap down," said his father. "Right here will be as good a place as any to leave it. Here's where the cattle sleep."

Mike and his father lifted the trap carefully to the ground. Jim Richards unfastened the hasps and opened the lid. Mike placed beef on biscuits and a piece of gooseberry pie on the trap floor.

"This pie will get him," Mike said.

After Mike had placed the food inside the trap, his father fastened the lid securely.

"Well, here it is," his father said. "We'll see in the morning whether or not this is a job well done."

"I'm glad tomorrow is Saturday," Mike said. "If we

catch him, I won't have to go to school. I'll be here to help bring him home!"

"Mike, I know you want the dog," Mr. Richards said. "But you must remember that his owner may be looking for him. If we capture him and you have to give him up later, it might hurt you, Son."

"I know that, Dad, but I want him anyway," Mike said. "I want to keep the dog as long as I can. I might get to keep him as long as he lives."

"I just want to warn you, Son, that you are taking a risk," his father explained. "If you take the dog and you have to give him up later, don't be surprised and don't let it hurt you."

"I'll try not to let it hurt me, Dad," Mike promised.

A HAPPY HOMECOMING

The red rooster's crow at four o'clock was the alarm for Lillian and Jim Richards to rise from bed and begin the new day. On school days Mike got up at six. But although this was Saturday morning, Mike was already wide awake, wondering if they had caught Speckles in the trap.

When he heard his mother and father getting out of bed, Mike got up, too. While his mother cooked breakfast, he helped his father feed and harness Bess and Doc. Then he and his father walked together through the morning starlight to the house for breakfast.

"Mike, you're up early this morning, and I know why!" his mother said.

"Yes, I can't wait to see if we caught Speckles last night!" the boy replied.

"Just as soon as we finish milking, we'll drive over to see," his father said.

Mike ate a bowl of hot cereal. Then he ate scrambled

eggs, bacon, and hot biscuits with golden butter and wild honey.

"Mom, this would be good bait to put in the trap for Speckles, too," he said. "This kind of a breakfast would catch him!"

"But I think we already have him in the trap, Son," said his father. "I don't see how we can miss with the kind of trap we have and the bait we're using."

Half an hour later Mike was sitting beside his father on the springy jolt-wagon seat with the leather lines in his hands, guiding Bess and Doc while they trotted across the pasture in the starlight. The fresh, cool, pine-scented wind made him very much awake at this early morning hour. Soon Mike drove the horses up near the cage and pulled stiffly on the lines. "Whoa, whoa, Bess and Doc! Whoa!" he said. The big horses understood and they came to a sudden stop.

"Dad, I can hardly wait to see if he's in the cage," Mike shouted. "Do you want to look?"

"No, you look first," Mr. Richards said.

Mike laid the lines across the seat. He stepped down from the wagon, with his father following a step behind him.

"Now, don't be afraid, Mike," said his father. "Walk up to the cage and look!"

Mike drew a deep breath and held it as he walked slowly toward the cage.

"He's in there, Dad!" Mike shouted. "He's in the cage! We have him! He's my dog! What will Junior Addington say now?"

"Take it easy, Speckles," Mike spoke softly. "We're not going to hurt you. We're going to give you a new home."

"Be careful, Mike," his father warned. "Don't put your face too close to the wire! We are strangers to him. Be easy with him at first. Be very kind and gentle. He might bite you through the wire!"

Mike moved back from the wire. He stood beside his father, looking down through the darkness at the indistinct figure of the hound. The dog cowered in one corner of the cage. He was trembling like a willow leaf in the April wind. They could see the rope around his neck with the end that he had dragged on the ground frayed like a frostbitten corn tassel.

"Well, we had better load the trap onto the wagon and haul him home," Mike's father said. "When the morning wears on, it will be lighter and we can have a better look at him."

"Dad, you can drive back," Mike said. "I'm going to stand beside the cage to watch my dog. I want to see him as soon as daylight comes."

"All right, Mike," said Mr. Richards, as they loaded the cage onto the wagon.

Mike jumped up beside the cage and stood looking through the woven wire at the dim outline of his captured dog. His father sat alone on the springy seat, guiding the trotting horses. They reached home just as dawn was breaking.

"Mom, we've got him!" Mike shouted, as he ran into the kitchen. "We've got Speckles! We caught him in that

cage Dad built! I want the best food you have for him to eat! And I want you to see him!"

Mike was so excited he could hardly talk. Small drops of perspiration formed on his flushed face.

"Mike, I'm happy that you've captured that hound," Mrs. Richards said. "I have plenty of good things here for him to eat!"

"I can hardly wait, Mom," Mike told her. "I want to talk to him. This morning I talked to him all the way across the pasture. Dad drove the team while I rode back beside the cage. I said to him: 'Speckles, you are my dog now. You'll never want for anything to eat. You'll have a good kennel to sleep in on cold winter nights. Speckles, you are my dog and I am your friend!' "

Mike's mother had found a half-dozen warm biscuits, two pork chops, some rich brown chicken gravy, and a large piece of fruit cake. She put these on a large platter for Mike to feed his hungry Speckles.

"We've got the cage in the woodshed, Mom," Mike said.

Mike ran ahead of his mother toward the woodshed. When she entered the shed with the food, Mike was looking through the cage, speaking softly to the hound.

"Mom, he's afraid," Mike said. "He shouldn't be afraid of Dad or you or me!"

When Mike's pretty mother walked up to the cage with the platter filled with food, she looked through the woven wire at the hound. He was crowded as far into the corner as he could get. He was still trembling with fear.

"Mom, I tell him not to be afraid, but he is!" Mike

said. "I don't understand it!"

"Maybe he doesn't understand how you feel about him, Mike," his mother said.

"If he doesn't understand now, he will after a few days," Mike replied.

Just then Mike's father appeared at the door.

"Lillian, what do you think of Mike's hound?" he asked. "Don't you think he's nice-looking?"

"I sure do, Jim," she replied. "But what makes him tremble so when he is with people who love him?"

"That's a hound dog's nature," Mr. Richards said. "He'll soon get over his fear. He doesn't like captivity, because he's used to freedom. He has been as free as the blowing wind!"

"I hate to see him in a cage," Mrs. Richards said. "I hate to see freedom taken from an animal that has always had it!"

"But Mom, we won't keep Speckles in this trap very long!" Mike said. "Just as soon as he gets used to us, we will let him go."

"We won't have to keep him locked up over three or four days," Mr. Richards said. "He will love us when he gets to know us. He will walk around this place like a king dog. And he will be the king dog here, for he will be the only one. He ought to be the happiest dog in the world!"

Mike and his mother and father stood close to the cage, looking at the shaking dog.

"First, we'll open the trap door and let him out in the woodshed," Jim Richards said. After we've left him in the woodshed awhile, he'll be tame enough for us to turn him loose to roam around the place."

"You sure think of the right things, Dad," Mike said.

"Get some water, Mike," Mr. Richards said. "Lillian, you set the plate of food on the floor. Then I'll let him out of the trap."

"Dad, I'd like to take that rope from around his neck," Mike said.

"Not now; you're a stranger to him," his father told him.

Mike's mother put the plate of food in the corner of the woodshed, where the windows were screened and there was plenty of room. Mike came in with a pan of water which he set near the food.

"Now, Mike, you and your mother go outside and close the door and I'll let him out," said his father.

Mike's mother waited at the door while Mike ran to the window and climbed up on a box so he could look inside.

He looked in just as his father opened the cage. He saw Speckles jump from the cage straight up in the air. When he came down on the concrete floor, he was running. He ran around the woodshed walls as fast as he could run a half-dozen times. Then he tried to climb the wall where he saw the April sky through a window. He didn't stop to eat the food or drink the water.

Mike's father opened the woodshed door, hurried through, and slammed the door shut behind him. Mike stepped off the box.

"That dog is really wild," Mr. Richards said to his wife.

29

"Mike will have trouble taming him. I think somebody has caught him before. They tied him up, but the dog escaped with part of the rope around his neck."

"Dad, he won't eat!" Mike said. "He's still running around the walls trying to escape!"

"We will have to go away and leave him alone," Mr. Richards said. "Maybe he'll settle down after a while and eat his food. Let's go away and leave him for a while. We can come back later to see what he is doing."

Mike climbed up on the box beneath the woodshed window again so he could watch Speckles. His father and mother stood near him.

"What's he doing now?" his father asked.

"He's still running around the wall," Mike replied. "He's the wildest dog I ever saw!"

"Dad, he's getting slower all the time," Mike said, after watching for a minute or two. "He's beginning to see it's no use to run around and around on the inside of this room. He knows he can't get out."

"He needs a little exercise," Jim Richards said. "Remember, he was just let out of a trap. I'm sure he was in it most of the night. Remember, he's had as much freedom as the wind has to run over these hills!"

"Now he's just walking around the walls," Mike said. "I believe he's going to stop!"

"Don't say anything to him, Mike," his father said. "He'll soon find out that we are his friends."

"Dad, he's stopped under the window," Mike said. "He's looking up at me. I know he wants to be my friend!"

Mike turned and looked down at his mother and father. There was a smile on his face now.

"When can I go inside where he is?" he asked. "Wouldn't it be safe to go now, Dad? He wouldn't bite me, would he? Not Speckles! He looks like he wants to be a friendly dog."

"Don't go in yet," his father warned. "He isn't calm enough to stop and eat his breakfast. Wait until after he eats his food."

"Now, do be careful, Mike," his mother warned.

"Don't you worry about me, Mom," he said.

31

Mike's mother and father walked away toward the house. They left Mike standing on the box looking down at the dog.

SPECKLES LISTENS

It was three weeks before Mike let Speckles out of the woodshed. Each morning and afternoon he went to the shed to feed, pet, and talk to the dog. By the time Speckles was turned out early in May, he knew this was his new home and that Mike was his new master. The hound seemed happy and contented.

Every morning when he saw the lights come on in the house, the dog got up, too. He came out of the kennel Mike and his father had built for him and went to the screen door of the house, where he stood wagging his tail. It wasn't hard for Mike to get up these mornings, either. He wanted to be at his regular place at the table where he could talk to Speckles through the screen door.

"Speckles, you will get your breakfast," Mike would say. "You must be patient. You understand my language, and I understand yours. You know what I am saying, don't you? I know that when you whine, you are asking me for something."

Speckles would push his nose harder against the screen. He would whine first, and then, when his sense of smell told him of the good things on the breakfast table, he would begin barking for his breakfast.

"Take it easy, Speckles!" Mike's father said one morning. "Mike's got his mouth full of honey and biscuit now. He can't talk to you. He'll be able to talk just as soon as he swallows his food."

"I am ready to talk, now," Mike said, after he had swallowed the last bite. "Speckles, you've been very patient. Now you will have your breakfast!"

The dog became very excited when Mike got up from the table. His eyes were brighter. They shone in the misty morning dawn as clearly as two bright embers.

"Wait just a minute," Mike told him.

"Get all the biscuits in the small pan," said his mother. "I put the pan in the warmer to keep the biscuits warm for him."

"That's the way to do it, Mom!" Mike said. "Speckles is like us! He likes his biscuits warm!"

Mike walked around the table to get the pan of biscuits.

"All right, now, Speckles," Mike said. "Mind your manners! I'll feed you!"

He pushed the screen door open and went outside. "Get ready, boy!" he said.

Mike picked up a biscuit and tossed it to Speckles. Speckles jumped high to catch it. One small bite and a quick swallow, and the biscuit was gone.

"A good catch, boy," Mike said. "Now, try this one!"

Mike threw another biscuit up, and the leaping dog caught it in his mouth. Then he threw another one, and another, and Speckles caught both of them.

"Now, Speckles, you can go down to the bus with me," Mike said, while he patted him on the head. "But don't you try to get on the school bus again!" "Dad," he told his father, who had stepped outside, "he got on the bus, and Henry Woodbridge had a time getting him off! I am glad he did, for Junior Addington got to see him. . . . There comes my bus! Good-bye, Dad!"

Mike hurried down the lane with Speckles beside him. The hound's tail curled up over his back as he ran.

"Speckles, you be here at four this afternoon to meet me," Mike's father heard him tell the dog. "Now be sure and be here!"

Mike and Speckles stopped when the school bus pulled up. The door opened and Mike got on.

The school bus was loaded with children. They looked from their windows and waved to Speckles, who wagged his tail and whined. Mike's hound watched the school bus go around the curve and out of sight. Then Speckles turned around and walked slowly up the lane toward the house, with his tail down as if he had lost his best friend.

The warm, sunny days of spring passed one by one. When the school year ended, Mike was very happy and Speckles was, too. When Mike went to the barn to help his father milk the cows and feed the horses, Speckles trotted along beside him. When Mike went with his father to cultivate the corn that grew up fast from the dark earth, Speckles went, too.

35

When Mike took his pole, line, and bait to Sandy River to fish, Speckles went with him. He sat beside Mike to watch him drop his line out into a deep hole where the big lazy fish played under the willows' shade. Everywhere Mike went, Speckles went, too.

"Now you are becoming Speckles' real master," Mike's father told him one evening. "Look how Speckles follows you! He never leaves you!"

Mike and his mother and father were sitting out in the lawn chairs under the wild plum tree in their front yard. They didn't need any shade from the plum tree, for the sun had gone down. There were long shadows over the house, barn, and countryside. Fireflies were little lanterns of gold moving about, lighting up the yard, garden, cornfields, meadows, and pasture fields. Dim stars had appeared in the high blue sky. They blinked

at Mike when he looked up at them through the wild plum leaves that were rustling in the gentle breeze. Speckles didn't look up through these green, rustling leaves at the stars. He sat close to the chair and looked up every time Mike moved.

"Yes, Dad, Speckles loves me," Mike said, smiling. "It is hard to believe now that he was once so wild we had to keep him in the woodshed!"

Mike had just spoken these words when Speckles jumped to his feet with his head thrust into the air. His nose was pointed toward a distant hill. His body was rigid, with his strong leg muscles bulging under the skin. He was alert, poised, and ready to go.

"Look at that dog's eyes, how bright they are!" said his mother. "I wonder what he sees!"

"Not one of us," said Mr. Richards. "He heard a familiar sound! That sound he heard must have stirred

old memories!"

"Wonder what it was, Dad?" Mike asked. "What is it, Speckles? Tell me what it is you hear!"

Mike put his hands on the dog's back. He stroked him gently. Speckles had always been pleased before when Mike did this, but now he stood as rigid as ever. He didn't seem to know anyone's hand was touching him.

"He is waiting for that sound again," Mr. Richards said.

Then, on that still summer evening, the Richards family heard a lonely fox horn start blowing on the distant hilltop. Speckles cocked his head to one side while he listened. There was one long toot, then three short ones. When Speckles heard them, his body became less taut. He relaxed while he put his nose in Mike's hand.

"Are you disappointed, fellow?" Mike's father asked Speckles. "Wasn't it the horn you thought it was? Are you still listening for the right horn? If you ever hear it, will you leave us and go?"

"Will he leave us, Dad?" Mike asked. "Do you think he will?"

"He loves you too much, Mike, to leave you," his mother said. "Who was ever better to a dog than you have been to him?"

"That doesn't make any difference," said his father. "Speckles is an exceptional dog. If we ever find out about him, I believe we'll find he's an outstanding foxhound. A great foxhound never forgets his master's call. He believed he heard his master's horn a while ago, but he was mistaken."

Now Speckles sat down beside Mike's chair. Mike tried to say something, but he couldn't.

He wouldn't leave me, he said to himself. Speckles wouldn't leave me.

"What if he had heard the right horn a while ago?" Mike's mother asked his father.

"He wouldn't be here now," Mr. Richards said. "There wouldn't have been any holding him. That's the nature of a good foxhound!"

THE TEST

The late September leaves had begun to turn color and tumble from the trees. One Friday afternoon when Mike came home from school, his father was waiting for him.

"Tonight will be a good time for us to see if Speckles will tree a possum," he said. "Tomorrow is Saturday and you don't have to go to school. If we stay up late hunting tonight, it won't matter."

"Dad, I'm ready to start any time," Mike said. "When will we go?"

"We'll go after we have done our chores and eaten supper," his father replied. "Since this is not possum-hunting season, if Speckles trees one, we'll have to leave it in the tree. We want to find out whether he trees possums or runs foxes!"

"Dad, can he do both?" Mike asked.

"Sure, he can," his father replied. "You play football, basketball, and baseball, don't you?"

"Sure, I do," Mike said proudly.

"Which one do you like best?" his father asked.

"I don't know," Mike replied. "I like all three."

"Well, that's the way with a hunting dog," Mr. Richards said. "I think maybe Speckles will like to chase foxes and tree possums, too. We can't ask him which one he likes to do best. But we can find out by taking him to the woods!"

Mike and his father did their chores by working together. By doing this, they could save time. When Mike forked down hay from the loft into the entry, his father forked this hay into the mangers for the horses, cows, and steers. When his father milked one cow, Mike milked the other. While his father used the separator, separating the cream from the milk, Mike carried the skimmed milk to the pen where he poured it into the trough for the hogs. When his father split kindling to start morning fires in the stove and fireplace, Mike carried it to the porch and filled the woodbox.

While Mike and his father worked in the barn, Mrs. Richards worked in the house. Since she knew they were going hunting, she got supper early. She baked an extra pan of hot biscuits for Speckles, too. When they had finished in the barn, she had supper ready for them. She had washed the lantern's smoked globe, trimmed the wick, and filled it with oil. She had lighted the lantern to see if it would give enough light for them in the dark woods. She knew starlight and moonlight couldn't penetrate the pine boughs that darkened the high slopes and deep valleys.

When they left the house, Mike's father carried the

lantern unlit. This was the time of day between sunset and darkness when the twilight was like a pale smoke covering the land. Mike's mother stood in the door, and proudly watched her son and husband walk across the orchard toward the distant hills. Mike was leading Speckles with a chain, while his father walked along with the lantern. She watched until the two were out of sight in the twilight.

"Dad, if Speckles will tree possums, would you care if I take him and go to the hills to hunt alone?" Mike asked.

"No, that would be the thing for you to do, Son," his father said. "When a young man grows up, he needs to be alone part of the time. Out under the moon and stars is a wonderful place for you to be! You need to be alone with your dog."

"We couldn't have chosen a better night to possum hunt," Mr. Richards said. "When there is wind in the leaves, it makes a noise that scares the possums. On a quiet, soft night like this, a possum likes to leave his den. He likes to go to a pawpaw patch or a persimmon grove to get something to eat."

The gray twilight had vanished and darkness had settled over the land when they reached the high hills.

"Here is the place to turn Speckles loose," Mike's father said. "If he'll tree possums, he can find them here."

Mike and his father stopped.

"While you turn Speckles loose, I'll light the lantern," Mr. Richards said. "The stars and moon won't give us enough light when we go up among the trees."

Mike unsnapped the chain from Speckles' collar, and the big hound took off in a run into the darkness, carrying his nose in the air.

"Will you know Speckles' bark when you hear it?" his father asked.

"Sure, I'll know it, Dad," Mike replied.

"Did you know a hunting dog has at least two different kinds of barks?" his father asked.

"No, I didn't know that," Mike replied.

"A dog has a running bark, and he changes it when he trees something," Jim Richards explained.

They climbed slowly up an old road that curved like a fence staple toward Laurel Ridge. Mike looked up into the sky at the stars.

"Wow, wow, wow!" a dog barked in the distance, loud and fast.

"That's Speckles, Dad!" Mike shouted. "That's my dog!"

Mike and his father stopped still in their tracks.

"That was a running bark," said his father. "He's on a red-hot track! Listen to him bark now! He's very close to whatever he's after!"

"There, his bark has changed!" Mike said.

"He's barking up a tree," his father explained. "That's his other voice. He's treed a possum!"

"Let's hurry, Dad!" Mike said. "He might leave the tree!"

"He won't if he's a good tree dog," his father told him.

"He must be a good tree dog, Dad," Mike said. "We've not been here five minutes and he's treed a possum!"

Mike began running in the direction Speckles was barking. His father ran ahead with the lantern, so he could light their way through the dark woods.

When Mike and his father emerged from the dark pine woods, they came into a field where there were only a few trees. Speckles had stopped barking.

"What do you think happened to Speckles, Dad?" Mike asked.

"I don't know," his father said. "Right about here is where he was just barking!"

"Yes, but he's gone now," Mike said. "Had I better

call him?"

"No, not yet," his father told him. "I'm going to shine the lantern light up into the trees. Maybe he treed something and left the tree. If he did, it's up in one of these trees, and if I shine the light up there on its eyes, they'll shine like little stars. Now, when I shine the light, you look up among the treetops for a pair of bright eyes!"

Jim Richards held the lantern above his head. The yellow glow of the light spread out among the brown leaves on the white-oak boughs. The light entered the little openings between the pine boughs laden with green needles and cones. The light spread only a few yards in all directions before it was closed in by walls of darkness.

"Do you see two eyes shining as brightly as little stars?" Mike's father asked him.

"No, I don't see them, Dad," Mike replied sadly.

"I wonder if Speckles treed anything at all," Jim Richards said. "But when I first looked at him in the pasture, I said to myself, 'He's an unusual dog. He's good for something.' But maybe I was fooled. Maybe he's not good for anything."

"Dad, I believe you are a good judge of dogs," Mike said. "Shine the lantern light back over on that little pine tree."

Jim Richards turned around and held the lantern higher so its soft yellow rays would go farther into the openings between the pine boughs.

"I see something bright, Dad!" Mike said. "I see two of them! They shine like stars!"

"I see them now!" his father said.

"I told you, Dad, you were a good judge of dogs!" Mike said.

Mike was excited now as he rushed over to the pine. He started looking straight up over his head at the two shining objects.

"It moved, Dad!" he shouted. "I think it's a possum!"

"But why didn't Speckles stay at the tree?" his father wondered. "A good tree dog never leaves the tree, Mike."

"It's coming down the tree, Dad," Mike said. "What could it be?"

"It's not a possum," his father said quickly. "Possums have a wild nature. They're afraid of people. They're even afraid of noises made by the wind rustling among the leaves."

Then Mike's father walked closer to the tree, holding up the lantern.

"It's a cat, Dad!" Mike said. "It's a friendly house cat, and he's rubbing his back on my legs. I wonder what he's doing here!"

"Out hunting, maybe," his father sighed. "Cats are

great hunters. They hunt miles away from home. Maybe he was chased here by dogs. A foxhound often gets fooled by a cat. The scent of a cat is a little like the scent of a fox!"

Mike was disappointed. He stood silently while the cat ran off into the dark woods.

"I don't believe Speckles is a tree dog, Mike," his father said. "These woods are good for possums. He's not barked again."

"Where do you suppose he is, Dad?" Mike asked. "Do you suppose he went back home?"

"He's out hunting for something, Mike," Jim Richards said. "He might be a mile away. If I am any judge of a dog, he has not gone home."

"Wow, wow, wow!" came the distant bark of a hound.

"Was that Speckles?" Jim Richards asked.

"That bark is so far away I can't tell," Mike said. "But I believe that's my dog, Dad."

"Well, if that's Speckles, he's after a fox!" his father said. "His barking is getting louder. He is coming this way!"

"Yes, Dad, that's Speckles barking!" Mike said. "Do you suppose I've got a foxhound?"

"If that's Speckles, you certainly have, and a good one!" his father answered.

Now Mike's father was getting excited.

"I've never heard a dog running a fox like that hound," Jim Richards said. "He is really driving him! Come, let's go to the top of Laurel Ridge so we can hear him!"

"Dad, do you like a foxhound better than a possum

hound?" Mike asked.

Mike was now running to keep up with his father, who had run back to the road that climbed up the steep side of the ridge.

"I like a foxhound," his father panted. "I wouldn't give a good foxhound for a dozen possum hounds!"

Mr. Richards was running up the wagon road that was made when timber had been cut and hauled down from Laurel Ridge. Mike was at his heels.

"He's bringing that fox this way," his father grunted. "If we get up on the ridge in time, we might get to see the fox!"

Mr. Richards was getting his breath very fast now. When they reached the top of the ridge, Mike was panting, too. Here the road leveled off and their running was easier. Mike caught up with his father and ran beside him.

"The fox crosses right out here by the rock cliffs," his father said.

"How do you know, Dad?" Mike asked.

They were breathing easier now.

"It's where they crossed when I fox-hunted here twenty years ago," Mr. Richards answered. "Foxes are a lot like people. The young foxes are taught by the old ones to do the same things they did. They steal chickens from the same farmers and cross the ridges at the same places!"

When Mike and his father reached the cliffs, they stopped.

"That's Speckles, Dad!" Mike said. "He's getting closer!"

"Don't talk, Mike," his father said. "Get behind that big pine tree. I'll blow out the lantern and stand behind this one. Don't say a word. The fox will run close enough for us to see him. And we can see the hound, too. We'll see if it's Speckles!"

Mike got behind a big pine tree. His father blew out the lantern and got behind another large pine.

"Don't breathe loud, Mike," his father whispered. "Hold back all you can. Don't make any noise."

They stood silently behind the two pine trees beside the cliffs. They heard the barking hound come closer and closer. Then they heard something's running feet, and a big red fox, with its long bushy tail floating on the wind, ran between the two pine trees. He didn't see Mike or his father. He ran on in the direction that Mike and his father had just come from.

Mike was so quiet he almost held his breath when the barking hound came running up from down under Laurel Ridge. His barking was short and fast when he came in sight. It was Speckles, all right. He ran between the two pine trees with his tongue out and his nose pointed into the wind. When Mike saw him, he looked like a speckled bundle flying through the wind. Mike couldn't see his feet touching the ground, and the dog was so close he could have reached out and touched him! In a half minute, Speckles had crossed Laurel Ridge and was going down the other side.

When Mike's father stepped out from behind his tree, Mike stepped out, too.

"You've got a really good foxhound, Mike," Jim

Richards said. "No, he's more than that—he's a great one!"

"Dad, I could have touched the fox with my hand!" Mike said. "I never saw a fox before! I could have touched Speckles, too! I didn't know he could run like that! I thought he had to put his nose on the ground to smell a track!"

"Not tonight, Mike," his father said. "The air is damp and the fox is hot. Speckles smells him on the wind! Listen to him now! He's so far away I can hardly hear him barking!"

"Dad, I like fox-hunting!" Mike said. "I got to see the fox and Speckles running really close to him! You knew the right place for us to wait to see the fox and the hound, too! Dad, this is great! How long will they run?"

"All night if the fox can stand it," his father replied. "That dog will never stop! Son, you have yourself a fox-hound! We might as well build us a fire and sit by it!"

"How long will we stay, Dad?" Mike asked.

"As long as he chases the fox," Mr. Richards replied. "I've seen a chase last all night and until noon the next day. I've seen the fox so tired he had to walk."

"Did the hounds catch him, Dad?" Mike asked.

"No, they were so tired they had to walk, too," Mr. Richards said.

"Where will we build a fire, Dad?" Mike asked.

"Right out here by Six Hickories is where we used to build a fire and listen," his father said. "I suppose they still build a fire there like we used to do."

Mr. Richards struck a match and lit the lantern. Mike followed him out the Laurel Ridge road.

"Dad, I don't hear Speckles now," Mike said.

"He is out of hearing now," his father said. "We'll hear him bringing the fox back in a few minutes."

Mr. Richards stopped.

"Here is the place," he said. "Sure, they still use it! Look at the pile of ashes! And somebody has left us some wood. Now I'll show you how to build a fire!"

Mr. Richards gathered a handful of dry leaves and placed them upon the ash pile. Then he laid fine twigs over the leaves. He placed sticks of wood the size of his thumb over the twigs. Mike held the lantern for him. Then Mike watched him strike the match to the leaves. He saw the tiny flame from the leaves first catch the twigs on fire. Then the flame from the twigs caught the thumb-sized sticks on fire. After these sticks begun to burn, Mike's father laid sticks as large as his leg onto the leaping flames.

"I can do that now, Dad," Mike said.

"Always be careful when you build an outdoor fire," Mr. Richards warned Mike. "Be especially careful in hunting woods. If our fire gets out and burns over the ground, it will end fox-hunting here for a long time."

"Why will it, Dad?" Mike asked.

"Dogs can't smell the track when the fox runs over the ground where fire has burned," his father replied. "The hound gets ashes in his nose. It hurts his sense of smell."

"I didn't know that," Mike said.

"Now we've got a good fire," his father said. "Let's sit on the side where the wind doesn't blow the smoke toward us."

Mike and Mr. Richards each got a block of wood to sit on. Mr. Richards blew the lantern flame out. Then he sat down on his block of wood beside Mike.

"Dad, I'm going to be a fox-hunter!" Mike said. "I love this!"

"Son, listen for your hound," his father said. "It's time for him to be bringing the fox back."

"Which way will Speckles come, Dad?" Mike asked.

"About the same way as he came before," his father answered. "The fox will run about the same circle all night."

"How long is the circle, Dad?" Mike asked.

"Ten or twelve miles," Mr. Richards replied.

"Really?" asked Mike. "Listen, Dad," he said. "I think I hear Speckles barking!"

Mike jumped to his feet. "I hear more than one dog!" he said.

"Sure you hear more than one dog! More and more hounds will join the chase, and by morning it will be something to hear!" his father told him. "Fox-hunters everywhere are out listening. They've turned their hounds loose, too, and some of them have good dogs. You will be hearing plenty about this chase and this new hound! Everybody will be wondering about Speckles. They will wonder whose dog he is and where he came from."

"I'm proud of my dog, Dad!" Mike said. "Listen how far ahead of the other dogs Speckles is!"

"He's a mile ahead!" Mr. Richards said proudly. "But it will take all night to decide this race. The hounds running behind now might be leading the pack in the morning!"

Mike sat back down on his block of wood to listen. He and his father became very still while Speckles chased the fox around the side of Laurel Ridge. They listened to him take the fox across Laurel Ridge by the cliffs and go down the other side until his barks became so faint they couldn't hear them. Mike counted seven more hounds in the chase. They were from a half-mile to a mile behind Speckles.

"Your Speckles is setting the woods on fire, Son!" his father said. "I've never heard one who could drive a fox like he can! Sparks must be flying from his feet!"

"When I go to school Monday I'll have something to tell, won't I, Dad?" Mike boasted.

"You sure will, Son," his father said.

After a while, Mr. Richards looked at his watch.

"It's twelve midnight," he said.

"We don't have to go home do we, Dad?" Mike pleaded.

"Not as long as Speckles runs that fox," his father told him. "I think we'll be up all night. Do you think you can stand it?"

"Sure I can, Dad," Mike answered.

Mike got up and laid more sticks of wood on the fire.

"We've got to have a fire, Dad," he said. "A wood fire is so pretty at night up here on this high ridge. I like to see the sparks go up!"

"Son, I know what you're talking about," his father said. "I've sat on this ridge at night beside a fire and listened to the hounds when I could reach up and take hold of a cloud. This is the prettiest place I've ever seen. I've seen the moon shine down on white clouds that covered the valleys. Laurel Ridge was an island among the clouds. I've seen the fox come up out of the clouds in the moonlight with a gang of barking hounds at his heels. It was the sweetest music I've ever heard. It is the only music I've remembered all my life. You'll like fox-hunting, Son! You'll make a great hunter!"

Mike and his father sat by the fire and listened until the wood burned low again. This time, Mr. Richards put more wood on the fire. One hour, then two, three, four, five, and six more went by while Speckles led a pack of more than twenty hounds. There were so many Mike couldn't count them.

Then streaks of light shot like long silver darts from the east. After the silver streaks of light, the big red sun peeped over the rim of distant hills. The world below Mike and his father was waking. Still the hounds kept running. They were much slower and their barks were shorter, but they kept on pursuing the tired fox.

"Foxes are smart," Mike's father said. "That old fox will go in a hole very soon. They don't like to run in daylight."

"Why is that, Dad?" Mike asked.

"They are afraid somebody will shoot at them," Mr. Richards said.

They mended the fire and listened to the chase for another hour. Suddenly, Speckles stopped barking. Mike and his father stood up and listened. Then, one by one, as the hounds reached about where Speckles had barked last, they stopped barking, too.

"That fox went into a hole," Jim Richards said.

"What will we do now, Dad?" Mike asked.

"We'll wait about thirty minutes," his father said. "Speckles will come limping in. He'll be tired for two or three days. We'd better start putting out the fire now, so a rising wind won't blow coals out in the dry leaves and set the woods on fire!"

"How can we do that, Dad?" Mike asked.

"We'll cover it over with dirt," Mr. Richards answered.

"We don't have any way to dig the dirt and shovel it," Mike said.

"We'll dig it up with sticks and use our hands for shovels," his father said. "Our hands are the best tools ever made!"

Before they had covered the fire over with dirt, Speckles came limping out the Laurel Ridge road.

"Speckles, you're tired," Mike's father said, "and you will have sore feet!"

Just then a horn sounded in the distance. Speckles held his head high and listened, looking as if he were ready to start running toward the sound.

"He's not too tired to listen to a horn!" Mr. Richards said.

After the horn had stopped, the hound dropped his head and limped closer to Mike.

Another horn blew in a different direction and he held his head high again to listen.

"He keeps listening for a horn," Mike's father said.

When the horn stopped, Speckles dropped his head again.

"He hasn't heard the right horn yet," Mr. Richards said.

"I hope he never does," Mike replied. The hound limped up and touched his leg.

"What a great dog!" Mike said, patting his head. "You led the pack all night, didn't you, Speckles?"

He put his arm around his dog's neck and pulled him up close.

"Son, you're a fox-hunter!" Mr. Richards said. "Now, we've got to get home and feed the livestock and milk the cows! We are going to be very late."

After they had smothered the fire with dirt, Mr. Richards got the lantern off the hickory limb where it had been hanging. He and Mike walked slowly toward home with Speckles limping behind them.

SPECKLES' CHOICE

On Monday when the school bus stopped at the end of the lane, Speckles was there waiting for Mike, in spite of his sore feet. Mike walked quickly up the aisle between the two rows of filled seats. He was carrying his books and coat and he was in a hurry to leave the bus.

"Hello, Speckles, boy," Mike said. "I'm glad to see you. You're my dog!"

The school bus moved slowly away while the other boys and girls watched Mike and Speckles from the window.

Mike laid his coat on the ground and put his books down on his coat. He put his arms around Speckles' neck and held him very close.

"I know you like me, Speckles, but you don't have to kiss my face!" Mike said, as the dog licked him.

When Mike let Speckles loose, the dog nuzzled his face again. Mike picked up his books and coat and went running up the lane with Speckles running ahead of him.

Speckles still limped on his sore feet, but he had his tail curled up over his back. Mike's father had said that when a foxhound curled his tail over his back, he was a happy dog.

This was the first time Mike had seen Speckles' tail curled over his back since the fox chase. Mike believed the hound hadn't walked proudly with his tail curled because his feet had been so painful when he walked on them.

"I had trouble on the bus this morning and at school today," Mike said to his parents as he entered the house.

"What kind of trouble?" his mother asked.

Mike never had trouble in school. He got along well with his classmates. His teachers liked him very much and he liked them.

"I had trouble over Speckles!" Mike said.

"How could you get into trouble over your dog?" asked his father.

"Junior Addington is trying to claim him!" Mike said. "He said his father lost Speckles in a chase last spring!"

"Did you tell him how we got Speckles?" Mr. Richards asked.

"Dad, I told him that long ago," Mike said. "He never claimed Speckles then. His father turned all five of his foxhounds into that chase Friday night. Speckles outran them. Now Junior and his father are trying to claim my dog!"

"Addington doesn't live five miles from here," Mr. Richards said. "If Speckles had been his dog, he would have gone home. Speckles used to belong to somebody.

But he couldn't have belonged to the Addingtons. They are not going to get him, either!"

"That is what I told Junior," Mike said. "I had planned to tell everybody about the fox hunt Friday night. But when I got on the bus this morning, Junior Addington was telling everybody about it! He was telling them about the great fox chase and how one of their dogs, the one we had stolen, had led about forty hounds all night! They were up all night, too, Dad, listening to the chase. They had a fire built on top of one of the Buzzard Roost Hills."

"I never heard of anything like that," Mike's mother said. "What do you think of that, Jim?"

"Freeman Addington had to pay a fine one time for stealing a foxhound," Jim Richards sighed. "Maybe you never heard about that. It happened a long time ago when he was a young fox-hunter. I was a young man and a fox-hunter, too. Freeman Addington is not going to steal Mike's dog! I'll see to that!"

"He's coming to see you about Speckles, Dad," Mike said.

"Who said he was coming to see me about Speckles?" Mr. Richards asked Mike. "Have you seen him? Did he tell you that?"

"Junior told me that at school today," Mike said. "Junior said his father wanted to look at Speckles to see if he wasn't the dog he lost last spring."

"Oh, that's different," Mr. Richards said. "He has not really claimed him yet. Sure, let him come, and we'll show Speckles to him! He will see that Speckles isn't his dog. And his son Junior might just be bluffing. He might not come at all."

"No, he wasn't bluffing, Dad," Mike said. "He meant what he said! They think we have their dog!"

"If they think that, they are wrong," Mr. Richards said. "When they come, I'll show Speckles to them. I'll treat them right. When I get through explaining to them, they'll know that Speckles doesn't belong to them!"

"Junior said they would be here one day this week," Mike said.

"The sooner the better," his father said.

"Dad," Mike said, "Junior Addington had better quit following me around at school and telling everyone I stole his dog. If he starts that again tomorrow, there is going to be more trouble!"

"Mike, we don't want any trouble," his mother said firmly. "Let's eat supper before it gets cold."

*   *   *

An hour later a pickup truck turned from the highway into the Richards' lane. Mike's mother, who was washing dishes in the sink by the window, saw the small, old-model truck. Mike watched it coming too, while he tossed bread, meat, and pie to Speckles and watched him catch it. Mike's father set his milk pails down when he saw the truck.

"There they come, Dad," Mike said, when the truck stopped. "I see Junior Addington in there! It must be his father with him."

"Yes, that's old Freeman Addington, all right," his father said. "I know him, but I don't know his son."

The truck doors swung open and a man and a boy got out just as Mike tossed Speckles a piece of apple pie. This was the last of his supper. Mike always gave Speckles the same dessert his mother had given him.

"That's the dog, Dad," Junior said. "That's the hound that outran our hounds last Friday night. Isn't he the one you lost?"

Freeman Addington was larger than Mike's father. He looked much older because his face was covered with a red beard. He also had a long red mustache that came out and curved down like horns. He wore a black hat slouched on the side of his head. He had on patched overalls and a faded shirt. He wore a jumper over his shirt that matched his overalls. His brogan shoes were turned up at the toes. He walked slowly toward Speckles and looked at him with his small blue eyes.

"Yes, that's our dog, all right," he said. "That's the dog I lost on Laurel Ridge about eight months ago!" he said.

"Well, if it isn't my fox-hunting friend of many years

ago," Jim Richards said. "'I haven't seen you for a long time, Freeman!"

"I heard about a hound you picked up in your pasture some time ago," Freeman said. "I've been very busy and never got around to paying you a visit to see if it was my dog. I lost a young dog about eight months ago on Laurel Ridge. I was up there hunting and had tied him with a rope. When Old Bell and Rodger struck a cold trail, he broke loose and took off with the rope around his neck. I never laid eyes on him again until now."

"Freeman, I don't believe you remember the dog you lost very well," Jim Richards said.

"You know better than that, Jim!" Freeman said.

"When one of us old fox- hunters once lays his peepers on a hound, he never forgets how he looks!"

"And we know the nature of a hound dog," Jim Richards told him. "We know he will find his real home if it is only five miles away. If this had been your dog, we could never have kept him here. He would have gone back to his real master if his home had been ten, twenty, fifty, or even a hundred miles away. Hound dogs swim rivers and travel miles to go back home after their owners have sold them. You know that, Freeman!"

"But you caught him in a cage, Jim," Freeman said, grinning. "You kept him closed up for three weeks. So he thought you were his master. When you feed a hound pie and cake, he will stay with just about anybody. I've always fed my hounds rough grub!"

"He's our dog," Junior said.

He looked over at Mike. His lips were tight and there was a frown on his face.

"He's not your dog *either*," Mike answered quickly.

"Mike, you let us settle this," his father said.

"Junior, you keep quiet and let me handle this," Freeman said. "Old Jim and I know one another. We might come to some agreement here since Jim doesn't fox-hunt any more."

"We don't have your dog, Freeman!" Jim Richards said firmly. "If I had thought he was your dog, I wouldn't have kept him!"

"Most anybody in these parts who has ever fox-hunted would like to keep a good dog," Freeman said.

"Only a very few men are dog thieves, Freeman," Jim

Richards said, looking right at the red-bearded man.

Freeman looked at Jim with his small blue eyes.

Mike sat down on the ground beside Speckles. He put his arm around his neck. Speckles licked his face.

"His name is not Speckles," Junior said to Mike. "His name is Scout."

"His name is Speckles," Mike said.

"Freeman, are you telling me the truth?" Jim asked him. "Does that hound really belong to you? Would you swear to that in court?"

"Yes, he is our dog," Junior said.

"You keep quiet, boy, and let your pap handle this," Freeman warned Junior. "Don't you speak up any more, boy, until I call on you!"

Junior looked down at the brown leaves that had fallen at his feet.

"Jim, he *is* my dog," Freeman answered in a softer tone. "Yes, I would swear in court that he is my dog!"

"Will he come to you when you call him?" Jim asked Freeman.

"He sure will," Freeman replied. Freeman looked at Mr. Richards for a minute.

"My boy Junior there can call that dog and he'd leave anybody and go to him," Freeman said.

"He won't leave me and go to Junior," Mike spoke up.

"He will, too," Junior said.

"A dog will go to his rightful owner, Jim," Freeman said.

Then Freeman twisted the horn of his red mustache while he looked at Jim Richards.

"There is a way to tell who he belongs to, then," Mike's mother spoke up. "Why not let the dog decide?"

"Would you be willing to turn the hound loose and let our sons call him and agree to let the one he goes to keep the dog?" Jim asked Freeman.

"What about that, Junior?" Freeman Addington asked. "Speak up, boy!"

"Well, yes, I would," Junior replied slowly.

"Would you be willing to do this, Mike?" his mother asked him.

"Yes, Mom," he replied quickly.

"Then, Junior, you go to that hill over yonder," Freeman said. "Boy, you go to that hill over here! Your pap and me will take Scout down in the valley between these little hills. We'll give you a signal to start calling before we turn him loose."

"You'll agree to this now, Freeman?" Jim Richards asked.

"On my honor, Jim," he replied. "Will you agree to it?"

"On my honor, I'll agree to it too," Jim replied.

"Junior, get to your hill right now, and when you hear the signal, you start calling," Freeman told his son.

"I'll go to my hill," Mike said.

"All right, we will hold old Scout," Freeman told them.

"What am I going to do?" Mike's mother asked.

"Mrs. Richards, you had better just stand here so you can see the hound go to Junior," Freeman told her.

"All right, I'll stand here," she told Freeman. "But, I'll never see Speckles go to your son! He'll never do that, Freeman Addington!"

69

Junior started running toward his hilltop. Mike went running toward his. These little hills were in a pasture field, and were covered with dry brown grass. Their summits were nearly two hundred yards apart.

"There's no trick to this, is there?" Freeman asked Jim Richards.

"No trick," Mr. Richards replied. "This is on the level. I'll put this chain on Speckles."

"There had better not be a trick!" Freeman warned him.

Jim Richards and Freeman Addington walked with Speckles between them down into the low meadow that separated the two little hills.

"Now, start calling!" Freeman shouted. "Call, Junior, as you never called before! We're fixing to turn Scout loose!"

"Here Scout, here Scout, here Scout!" Junior shouted.

"Here Speckles, here Speckles, here Speckles, here!"

Mike called.

Jim Richards unsnapped the chain from the dog's collar. Mrs. Richards watched from the nearby slope. Both boys were calling the foxhound at the tops of their voices. The hound stood for a minute with his nose pointed in the air. He turned his head first one way and then the other.

Then Speckles started toward Mike so fast that all four of his feet looked as if they were off the ground. He looked as if he were running on the wind. Mike kept on calling as Speckles ran toward him.

"Ah, shucks!" Freeman Addington said to Jim Richards. "We must have got him mixed up with the dog we lost. He looks so much like our dog! I guess we made a mistake!"

When Junior saw Speckles running up the hill to Mike, he stopped calling. Mike's mother clapped her hands and laughed with joy. When Speckles reached Mike, he gathered the dog up in his arms.

"Are you satisfied now, Freeman?" Jim Richards asked.

"Well, I guess I am," the big man replied. "I agreed to this test of ownership. I guess after you keep a hound eight months and feed him hot biscuits, pie, and cake, he might change his mind about his real owner who had to feed him plain old rough grub!"

"A good hound knows his rightful owner, Freeman," Mr. Richards said. "You have owned enough hounds and fox-hunted long enough to know that."

Freeman Addington didn't listen to Jim Richards' last words. He was on his way back to his truck. Junior had already climbed in it. Mike came walking proudly down the slope with Speckles.

"Now we know the rightful owner, don't we?" he said. "Junior Addington will stop talking now, won't he?"

"We know that Speckles doesn't belong to the Addingtons," his father said. "But his real owner could still turn up."

"Mike, I'm so proud that Speckles went to you," Mrs. Richards told her son.

THE RIGHTFUL OWNER

A few weeks later, Mike and his father sat on a log before a fire on Laurel Ridge. They were listening to the sweet music of the barking hounds. The sweetest music of all came from Speckles. He was way out in front of the pack as they circled back to Laurel Ridge.

"Dad, this is great!" Mike said. "Listen to Speckles, won't you? He's a hound dog I am proud to call my own!"

"He's a great dog, Son," his father said.

Mike got up from the log to lay more pine boughs on the fire. When he laid the dry boughs over the red embers, the flames leaped up. Sparks leaped higher than the flames and disappeared on the night wind.

"Listen to that music, Dad," Mike said. "Did you ever hear anything prettier than hound-dog music on a bright October night?"

"No, I never have, Son," his father replied.

Then Mike stood on his tiptoes and reached as high

as he could toward a white cloud floating over Laurel Ridge.

"I can almost reach it, Dad," he said.

Above this white cloud was a night sky with a big, bright moon and many stars.

"I've had more fun fox-hunting than I ever had in my life," Mike said. "I like to be up high on Laurel Ridge where I can reach for a cloud or a star and listen to the music of the barking hounds! I love fox-hunting on October nights!"

"Stop talking now, Mike, so the fox will come closer," his father whispered. "You'll get to see Speckles close behind him!"

Then, very suddenly, Speckles stopped barking.

74

"I wonder what's wrong, Dad," Mike said. "Do you suppose he's caught the fox?"

"I don't know what has happened," his father answered.

Mr. Richards jumped up from the log. He and Mike were silent while they listened.

"What's wrong, Dad?" Mike asked again.

"I don't know," his father replied. "This is very strange! Nothing like this has ever happened before!"

The pack of barking hounds were nearly at the spot where Speckles had last barked.

Then there was a loud blast from a hunter's horn about two hundred yards away. Its lonesome call was louder than the music of the hounds. There was one long lonesome call, followed by seven short ones.

"What does that mean, Dad?" Mike asked.

"Let's go and see," his father said.

Mr. Richards took the lantern down from where it was hanging in a tree. He lifted the globe and lighted it with a piece of pine bough. Then he hurried in the direction where they had heard the horn. Mike was already running ahead.

Suddenly they heard a man's voice.

"I heard you leading the chase, Rags," the man said. "But you scented me on the wind and you were on your way to me before I blew my horn!"

"Do you hear that, Dad?" Mike asked.

"Yes, I hear," his father said.

They stopped only a few feet from where the man was talking to a dog in a choked voice.

"He called to a dog named Rags, Dad," Mike said. "He can't be talking to Speckles!"

"He might be," his father replied. "That might have been the horn Speckles has been waiting to hear. I never heard it here before."

"Dad, if he is the rightful owner, I don't know what I'll do," Mike said. "I don't believe I can give Speckles up to anyone!"

"If he's the rightful owner, you must be brave, Son," his father told him. "We'll soon see!"

As Mike and his father walked around a turn in the Laurel Ridge path, their lantern light flashed on the man and dog. It was Speckles. He was leaping up, trying to lick the man's face.

"Be a brave boy, Mike," his father whispered. "You must be braver than he is. He is almost crying."

Just then the man saw Mike and his father. "Rags has been gone since last March," he said. "Now I've found him! I've found him! I can't believe it!"

"My name is Jim Richards," Mike's father said. "And this is my son Mike. We've had this dog since last April."

"My name is Tom Adams," the man said, as he put Speckles back on the ground to shake hands with Jim Richards.

"I'm very glad to see you, Mr. Richards," Tom Adams said.

When Tom Adams turned to shake Mike's hand, Speckles was standing with his front paws on Mike's shoulders. Mike was stroking his face gently.

"I hate to lose you, Speckles," Mike said softly. "You hate to lose me too, don't you?"

"Where did you find him, Mike?" Tom Adams asked.

"In the cow pasture last April with a rope around his neck," Mike replied softly.

"How did you lose him?" Mike's father asked.

"Well, Mr. Richards, we jumped a fox in Carter County," Tom Adams said. "The fox ran away with a pack of hounds behind him. All the hounds came back but Rags. I've been everywhere in Carter County hunting for him. I've also been over most of your Greenwood County. I have traveled hundreds of miles, blowing my horn on the ridges and hilltops. I knew if he ever heard this horn, he would come! A good hound never forgets his rightful owner! And Rags is the best hound I've ever owned. I have fox-hunted since I was your son's age and I've owned many dogs."

"We love your dog, too," Jim Richards said. "I used to fox-hunt when I was a young man. When Mike and I took him hunting the first night and I heard him run a fox, I said he was one of the best I had ever heard!"

Now Speckles had taken his paws off Mike's shoulders. Tom Adams shook Mike's hand.

"Mike, I'm glad to meet you," Tom Adams said. "You saved my dog! I don't know what the rope was doing around his neck, but that was dangerous. He might have got hung up and died."

Tom Adams was older than Mike's father. His face was covered with a long, gray beard. He was a tall man,

and age had bent him like a tree. His hands were big
and rough like Mike's father's hands. He wore overalls,
a torn coat, a slouched hat, and scratched boots.

"Mike, I hate to take him from you," Tom Adams
said. "I know he has learned to love you because you
have been kind to him."

"Mr. Adams, I love him very much," Mike said. "But
I know he is your dog!" Mike could feel the tears trickle
from his eyes down his face, but he wouldn't let himself
cry.

"I called him Speckles, Mr. Adams," he said. "If he
ever forgets the name Rags, you just call him Speckles!
See if he won't come when you call him by that name!"

"Mike has fed him good food and loved him, Mr.
Adams," Mike's father said. "Your dog has had the same
food we ate from our table."

"Do you like to fox-hunt, Mike?" Tom Adams asked.

"Yes sir, I love it," Mike replied bravely. "Speckles taught me to love fox-hunting!"

"Mike," Tom Adams said, "I owe you something for keeping my dog. How much money shall I pay you?"

"None," Mike replied. "Speckles has already paid me! He paid me with his love and by leading the chase! I'll know his bark now whenever I hear it!"

"Mike, I want to pay you something," Tom Adams said. "Now, I have other foxhounds. Four of them are young hounds. They are Rags' sons. One looks just like Rags. I want to give him to you. I can sell this dog for over a hundred dollars! But I want to give him to you for keeping Rags this long for me."

"Oh, that's wonderful!" Mike said. "I'll call him Speckles! What do you think, Dad?"

"I think that's great, Mike!" his father said. "Mr. Adams is a very fair man!"

"Dad, when can we go after him?" Mike asked.

"I'll bring him to you," Tom Adams said. "You live down in this valley, don't you?"

"Yes sir," Mike said. "We live in the first house on the lane up from the hard road."

"I'll bring your dog tomorrow," Tom Adams said. "I know how lonesome a man can be without a hound dog."

"Oh, thank you!" Mike said.

"I must be going," Tom Adams said. "I must take Rags back to his old home. I have my car waiting at the foot of Laurel Ridge on the Sandy River road."

"We have to go back, Mike, and cover the fire," his

father said gently.

Mr. Adams shook hands again with Mike's father. Then he walked slowly away. For a minute, Speckles stood between them. He didn't want to leave Mike.

"Go with your owner," Mike told him. "I'll see you again, Speckles!"

"Come, Rags," Tom Adams called.

The pretty hound looked up again at Mike. Then he turned and slowly followed Tom Adams away, while Mike stood there watching them go out of sight.

"Come on, Son," Mike's father said. "Let's go cover the fire."

Mike and his father walked silently back to the fire. Mr. Richards dug up dirt with a stick while Mike threw it on the fire with his hands. Not a word was spoken while they did this. In the last fading flickers of light from the fire, Mr. Richards could see the tears running down Mike's face. After they had put the fire out, they walked toward home. They walked in silence for over a mile.

"Mike, we know where Speckles is now," his father said. "When you want to go see him, I'll take you!"

"That will be fine, Dad," Mike said. "I'll want to see him again. But I will have a Speckles of my own, too, that nobody can take. He'll always come to me because I'll be his rightful owner!"

About The Author

Jesse Stuart (1906-1984) was one of America's best-known and best-loved writers. During his lifetime he published more than 2,000 poems, 460 short stories, and nine novels. His more than 60 published books include biography, autobiography, essays, and juvenile works as well as poetry and fiction. These books have immortalized his native hill country.

Stuart also taught and lectured extensively. His teaching experience ranged from the one-room schoolhouses of his youth in eastern Kentucky to the American University in Cairo, Egypt, and embraced years of service as school superintendent, high school teacher and high school principal. "First, last, always," said Jesse Stuart, "I am a teacher. . . . Good teaching is forever, and the teacher is immortal."

Stuart wrote eight books for young people. The Jesse Stuart Foundation, a non-profit organization devoted to preserving the legacy of Jesse Stuart, is making these books available to a new generation of readers. *A Penny's Worth of Character, Hie to the Hunters, A Jesse Stuart Reader, A Ride With Huey the Engineer,* and *The Beatinest Boy* have recently been re-issued. *The Rightful Owner* will be followed by a biography of Jesse Stuart for young readers.

Illustrated by Robert Henneberger, a graduate of the Rhode Island School of Design. Book design by Rocky Zornes, of ZAK Productions, Lexington, Kentucky.

THE JESSE STUART FOUNDATION

The Jesse Stuart Foundation was founded in 1979 as a public, non-profit entity devoted to preserving both Jesse Stuart's literary legacy and W-Hollow, the little valley made famous in his works. The Foundation controls the rights to Stuart's works, and it is reprinting Stuart's out-of-print books at the rate of 4 per year.

The 730-acre Stuart farm in W-Hollow, exclusive of the home place, was turned over to the Commonwealth of Kentucky by the Stuarts in 1980. It is now designated the "Jesse Stuart Nature Preserve" and is part of the Kentucky Nature Preserves System, with ownership vested in the Kentucky Nature Preserves Commission. The Jesse Stuart Foundation has the responsibility of operating the Preserve, and is developing a management plan which will ensure the preservation of W-Hollow. The valley has been made memorable in Stuart's works, and his soil and water conservation practices and protection of wildlife have made it into both a model of fertility and a wildlife refuge. It will now serve permanently as a reminder to visitors of Jesse Stuart's conviction of America's need to preserve her natural resources. A trail system is also being developed to make it possible for visitors to see the places in the valley which are portrayed in Stuart's stories and novels.

The Jesse Stuart Foundation is governed by a Board of Directors consisting of University presidents, members of the Stuart family, and leaders in business, industry, and government. The Foundation also has an Executive Director, who manages the day-to-day business, plans and schedules events and meetings, coordinates publication projects, and edits a quarterly Newsletter.

Associate Memberships in the Foundation are available to the general public. Associate Members will receive the Newsletter, and a Stuart book or print as a membership gift. The following categories of associate membership are available, with the annual fees as indicated:

Senior Citizen or Student	$ 10
Single	$ 15
Family	$ 25
Patron	$ 50
Benefactor	$100

A Life Membership is also available at a cost of $500. Those who donate $1,000 or more to the Foundation are designated "Guardians of a Storied Past."

For more information, contact:

The Jesse Stuart Foundation
P.O. Box 391
Ashland, KY 41114
(606) 329-5232

NEED FOR JESSE STUART'S JUVENILE WORKS

It is vitally important that American youth be presented with the notion that uncompromising commitment to high standards is the best personal philosophy. Jesse Stuart's books are a guideline to the solid values of America's past. With good humor and brilliant storytelling, Stuart implicitly praises the people of Kentucky whose quiet lives were captured forever in Stuart's wonderful novels and stories. In Stuart's juvenile works, youngsters will find people who value hard work, who love their families, their land, and their country; who believe in education, honesty, thrift, and compassion—people who play by the rules.

Today, we are so caught up in teaching children to read that the process has obscured the product. Children require more than literacy. They need to learn, from reading, the unalterable principles of right and wrong.

That is why Stuart's children's books are so important. They allow educators and parents to "kill two birds with one stone." They make reading fun for children, and they teach solid values in the process.

In a world that is rapidly losing perspective we must provide books that will truly educate tomorrow's adult citizens and leaders.

OTHER BOOKS BY JESSE STUART

For readers in grades 3-6

A Penny's Worth Of Character
$3 softback/$10 hardback

A Ride With Huey The Engineer
$6 softback/$12 hardback

The Beatinest Boy
$5 softback/$10 hardback

For readers in grades 7-12

Hie To The Hunters
$20 hardback

A Jesse Stuart Reader
$20 hardback

Split Cherry Tree
$3 softback

Jesse Stuart, The Boy From The Dark Hills
$15 softback

The Jesse Stuart Foundation
P.O. Box 391
Ashland, KY 41101
(606) 329-5233

Adult Education

We live in a world of ever increasing technology. Jobs have become more complex, and they require more formal education and training. Consequently, a good education is essential to survival and success in today's society.

Opportunities for more education are available in your local communities; in fact, with the help of Kentucky Educational Television, you can study at home. Brief descriptions of some of the programs available are listed below:

Kentucky Educational Television (KET)
(Call 1-800-432-0951)

KET allows adults at any level of ability to study at home. Whether you do not read at all and need to "Learn to Read," want to get a "G.E.D. on T.V.," or let college come to you, KET has a program which can benefit you.

Kentucky Department of Education (KDE)
(Call 1-800-372-7179)

The Department of Education helps adults learn to read, to improve their basic skills, and to receive a G.E.D. All Adult G.E.D. classes are offered free of charge in local schools or other public facilities.

KDE also sponsors community education programs. Courses range from auto mechanics to foreign languages to real estate.

AFTERWORD

For the fourth year, the Kentucky Jaycees and the Jesse Stuart Foundation are distributing copies of a Jesse Stuart book to sixth graders throughout the state. The purpose of the 1991 Jesse Stuart Book Project is to put a copy of *The Rightful Owner* in the hands of as many Kentucky sixth graders as possible, in the hope that the story will encourage them to read for pleasure and thus help them to stay in school. It will also promote interest in Kentucky history and literature.

Jesse Stuart once remarked that "If the United States can be called a body, Kentucky can be called its heart." He was speaking metaphorically, of course. But the Jaycees' work on the Jesse Stuart Book Project certainly adds another dimension to the word "heart," and also exemplifies Stuart's own statement, "No joy runs deeper than the feeling that I have helped a youth stand on his own two feet, to have courage and self-reliance, and to find himself when he did not know who he was or where he was going."

If you would like to contribute to the Jesse Stuart Book Project, please send your check to Mr. C.J. Johnson, 110 Sundown Road, Grayson, KY 41143. Every $1.50 that you contribute places a treasured book in the hands of a Kentucky child.

Ms. Judy B. Thomas
Chairperson, Jesse Stuart Foundation